Copyright © 2009 Jenny Alexander
Illustrations copyright © 2009 Mark Oliver
Reading consultant: Andrew Burrell, MA, PhD

First published in Great Britain in 2009
by Hodder Children's Books

The right of Jenny Alexander and Mark Oliver to be identified as the Author and
Illustrator of the Work has been asserted by them in accordance with
the Copyright, Designs and Patents Act 1988.

1

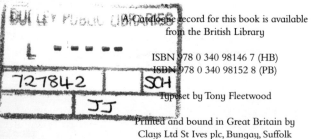

A Catalogue record for this book is available
from the British Library

ISBN 978 0 340 98146 7 (HB)
ISBN 978 0 340 98152 8 (PB)

Typeset by Tony Fleetwood

Printed and bound in Great Britain by
Clays Ltd St Ives plc, Bungay, Suffolk

The paper and board used in this book are natural recyclable products made from
wood grown in sustainable forests.

Hodder Children's Books
a division of Hachette Children's Books
338 Euston Road, London NW1 3BH
An Hachette UK company
www.hachette.co.uk

CAR-MAD JACK

The Versatile Van

Written by
JENNY ALEXANDER

Illustrated by
MARK OLIVER

A division of Hachette Children's Books

· CHAPTER 1 ·

Jack Davy was mad about cars – he was the most car-mad boy in the world! He was also the luckiest boy because his Dad and Uncle Archie ran the car supermarket on the edge of town. Every Saturday, Jack spent the morning there. He counted the days. He couldn't wait!

One Saturday, Jack woke up feeling even more happy than usual. It was the day after his birthday. Ten friends had come to his party. They had brought him ten presents. Jack looked at all his presents lined up on the floor beside his bed.

There was a car-shaped alarm clock that went 'beep beep' instead of 'ring ring' and some toy traffic lights that really lit up. There were three pairs of racing car socks and a computer game called *Hit the Gas and Go!* A lunchbox shaped like a London bus. An ambulance with back doors you could open.

There was a pack of Car Facts Top Trump cards. Five books in a box called Ace Racing Drivers. A family ticket to Digger-world and a set of colouring pencils in a car-shaped pencil case.

Jack got dressed. He put on a pair of new socks. They looked great. He picked up the pencils – he could take them to the car supermarket and make a new poster for 'Jack's Wall of Cars'. All his other presents would be there for him to play with when he got home. It was going to be a brilliant day!

He bounded down the stairs. Dad had already left for work but everyone else was in the kitchen, having breakfast.

'Good morning, Jack,' said Mum.

'Dak! Dak!' said Nico, banging his spoon.

'Woof!' said Porridge, thumping his tail.

Amber looked up and scowled at Jack.
She was still in a bad mood. She never
liked it when someone else had a birthday,
so they all knew that yesterday would be a
Grumpy Day. They just didn't know how
long it would last. Amber's grumpy moods
were like thick sticky mud. Sometimes she
could get stuck in one for weeks.

Amber was wearing her pink leotard, tights and fluffy white top, ready for ballet. As Jack sat down, she glared at his feet in their fancy new socks. She swung her own feet out from under the table.

'Jack's got brand new socks,' she grumbled. 'And all my tights have got holes in!'

'That's only a tiny hole,' said Mum. 'No one will see it when you've got your ballet shoes on. Now eat your breakfast, both of you. We don't want to be late.'

Jack helped himself to some Weety-bites.

Amber stuck out her bottom lip. She poked at the cornflakes in her bowl.

'These cornflakes have gone soggy,' she grumbled. She dumped her bowl on Nico's tray.

'Me no want Ammer cornplakes!' said Nico, pushing the bowl away with his pudgy little hands.

He kept pushing. He pushed it right over the side.

Bang! The bowl hit the floor next to Porridge's nose.

Splash! Soggy cornflakes splattered all over him.

Woof! Porridge sat up in his basket and started to lick them off.

Mum frowned at Amber.

'I think you had better get a cloth and

clean that up,' she said.

'Why should I?' said Amber. 'Nico did it,
not me!'

Mum sighed.

'Just have some toast and try to stop
grumbling,' she said.

While Mum was cleaning up the
cornflakes Amber helped herself to toast.

'This toast has gone cold!' she grumbled.

She put some butter on it and started grumpily munching.

'All ready for the car supermarket?' Mum asked Jack, taking no notice of Amber.

'Yes, I can't wait,' he said, excitedly. 'I'm going to take my new pencils and make a poster.'

Amber made a noise that sounded like 'Loser!' but she might have just been choking on a crumb.

Jack was fed up of listening to Amber's grumps and grumbles. He wished Mum and Dad would tell her off, not just ignore her. Sometimes he said so. 'Why do you let her be so grumpy all the time?' he would ask.

Then they would shrug their shoulders. 'She'll grow out of it,' they would answer. 'It's just her age.' But Jack knew that wasn't

true or else all the girls in Year 6 would
be moody and rude like Amber, and they
weren't.

Secretly, Jack believed Amber wasn't
a normal girl at all. She was an Alien
from Planet Grumpy. 'There are two
brilliant things about Saturday mornings,'
he thought. 'One is that I go to the car
supermarket. The other is that Amber the
Alien doesn't.'

It seemed like ages before they were ready to leave. First Mum had to find some ballet money for Amber. Then she had to change Nico's nappy. Amber had to clear the table and Jack had to put the dishes in the dishwasher.

As they were getting into the car Nico filled his nappy and Mum had to go back inside and change Nico's nappy again.

'I wish I was an only child,' grumbled Amber.

At last, they arrived at the car supermarket. Jack noticed the top of a gleaming white van above the roofs of all the other cars for sale. He had never sat behind the wheel of a big van.

He jumped out of the car as Dad came out to meet him.

'Can you show me that white van?' Jack asked, grabbing Dad's arm.

'Of course!' said Dad. He ruffled Jack's hair. 'Let's just wave the others off first.'

They waved as Mum drove slowly out on to the road. Mum waved back. Nico waved back. Amber stared straight ahead with a face like thunder.

'I'm going to be late for ballet. Again!' she grumbled.

· CHAPTER 2 ·

Jack and Dad walked round the outside of the tall white van. It had a wide sliding door on the pavement side for loading things. It had a Ford badge on the front and 'Transit' in silver letters on the doors at the back. It was the biggest vehicle they had ever had for sale in the car supermarket.

'Wow!' said Jack. 'It's really big!'
He couldn't wait to climb up inside.

Dad laughed.

'Ford invented the Transit van more than forty years ago,' he told Jack. 'It was the very first van that was built to drive like a car. Before that, vans were more like boxes on wheels.'

Forty years! Jack couldn't imagine it. Even Mum and Dad weren't around that long ago.

'They've sold more than five million Transits now,' said Dad. 'Not all the same model of course – there are lots of different Transit models.'

Five million! Jack couldn't imagine that either.

Dad unlocked the back doors and opened them wide. The back of the van was big and empty. It had a bare metal roof and dark-grey rubber matting on the floor. One of the walls was lined with wood. There were three shelves on it, covered in splashes and circles of paint.

Jack clambered up inside. He could stand up! He could jump around!

'This is so cool!' he said.

His voice echoed in the hollow empty space.

Just then, a customer came and asked
Dad if he could test-drive the Mitsubishi
that was 'Car of the Month'.

'Will you be all right for a few minutes,
Jack?' asked Dad.

Jack grinned and nodded. He watched his dad and the customer go off to the office to get the keys. He sat down on the floor in the back of the van. It didn't have the car smell of carpets and polish. It smelt of wood and metal and paint.

'I wish I had a van like this,' thought Jack.

He imagined all the things he could do if he had a Ford Transit van. He could go on a huge shopping trip and buy everything he wanted. He could get a racing-car bed and a climbing frame and a trail bike – it would all fit in! Then he could take everything he didn't want to the dump.

The van was so big, he could have a birthday party in it. He could make it into a playroom for Nico and Porridge. He could turn it into an ice-cream van, or a camper van, or a mobile sweet shop.

When his dad came back, Jack told him all the ideas he had thought of.

'Yes,' said Dad. 'The Transit is a very versatile van.'

'Versatile?' said Jack.

'You can use it in lots of different ways,' Dad explained. 'Would you like to take

a look inside the cab?'

Jack jumped down and they went round to the driver's door. The seat was too high up for Jack to see right across the cab. He climbed in. He sat in the driver's seat and looked at all the buttons and dials.

The cab was roomy and wide. It had a wall behind the seats so that you couldn't see into the back. The passenger seat was big enough for two people and it had two seat belts.

'The last owner was a painter and decorator,' Dad said. 'He needed a big van to carry his paint tins and ladders.'

'Do you think another painter and decorator will buy it now?' asked Jack.

'Maybe,' said Dad. 'Or maybe a removals company – they could use it to shift furniture. Or a delivery person could use it to deliver bread to a baker's shop or flowers to a florist's.'

Jack tried to imagine delivering flowers or furniture in his Ford Transit van but it didn't feel very exciting just moving things around.

'Who else might buy it?' he asked.

Dad scratched his chin. 'Well, builders sometimes drive Ford Transits – they have to use big bags of cement and heavy tools. Or gardeners – they could put their lawnmowers and compost and hedge-cutters in the back.'

Dad said that anyone who used heavy tools or machines for their work might drive a Transit van. Carpenters, electricians, plumbers ...

Jack grinned. He had a great idea for a pretend game.

'I've got to go in and do some paperwork now,' said Dad. 'Would you like to stay out here for a while?'

As if he needed to ask!

When Dad had gone, Jack put his hands on the steering wheel. He could see right

over the tops of all the other cars. He was Jack Davy, the plumber. It said 'JD Plumber' in big letters on the side of his van. In the back, he had his heavy bag of tools. He had a bundle of water pipes strapped to the wall, and boxes of taps and washers on the shelves.

The only time Jack had seen a plumber at work was when one came to fit the new bathroom at home. He imagined he was going to fit a new bathroom. He had the new bath and toilet and sink in the back of his van. He started to back slowly out of the car park. It was hard to steer the big van out of the narrow parking space but Jack was a good driver. He was proud of his driving skills.

The main road was choked with traffic.

It was stop, start, stop, start all the way.

'Maybe this wasn't such a good idea,' Jack thought, as he came to another red light.

Then suddenly, his mobile phone rang. He pulled over to answer it.

'Is that Jack Davy the plumber?' said a panicky voice.

'Yes.'

'Well this is an emergency, please come quick!'

'Where are you?' Jack asked. 'What's the trouble?'

'I'm outside a house in Merrivale Road.'
Merrivale Road ... Jack didn't know where
that was.

The caller said, 'I saw water pouring out
from under the front door so I knocked,
but nobody answered. I looked through
the letterbox. There must be a burst pipe
because the whole house is flooded.'

Jack imagined the flooded hallway. He
imagined the flooded living-room.

'And there's something else,' the caller
said. 'I think there's a rabbit trapped inside!'

Jack imagined the flooded kitchen. There
were saucepans floating out of cupboards.
There were packets of food bobbing about
like boats. Right in the middle, he saw the
poor rabbit, sitting on the roof of its hutch.
The water was lapping around it.

Jack's best friend, Sandor, used to have a rabbit that lived in the kitchen. The whole family adored it. When it caught a chill and died, everyone cried and cried. He couldn't let the family with the flooded house lose their rabbit.

He had to get there quickly! He had to rescue that rabbit!

· CHAPTER 3 ·

Luckily, the van had a sat nav. Jack keyed in where he was on the High Street and 'Merrivale Road', where he needed to be. The map showed a short-cut through some side streets. 'That's good,' thought Jack, because it would take all day if he had to stay on the busy main road.

The sat nav told him to turn left into Oak Trees Road, so he signalled, slowed down and turned. He couldn't see any oak trees, just a solid line of cars parked along each side of the road. The gap in the middle was hardly wide enough for the big white van to get through.

Plumber Jack had to steer very carefully but at least he kept moving. He didn't have to stop and start all the time for traffic lights and crossings.

'This is better,' he thought.

But then ...

Oh, no! There was a huge rubbish lorry blocking the road ahead. It was moving very slowly, slower than walking pace. Two men wearing orange jackets and thick rubber gloves were following behind. They were picking up the rubbish bags from outside the houses and tossing them into the back of the lorry.

Jack jammed on the brakes. All he could

think about was the poor rabbit.

He beeped his horn. The rubbish men
ignored him. They just went on picking up
the black bags and tossing them in.

Jack beeped the horn
again. He kept his hand
on it. This time the bin
men looked round. One
of them came over to talk
to him.

'What's the hurry,
mate?' he said.

'It's an emergency!' Jack
told him. 'I'm a plumber and I've got to
get to a house that's flooding. There's a pet
rabbit trapped inside!'

The bin man sprang into action. He ran
round the side of the rubbish lorry and

shouted up to the driver.

'This van's got to get past,' he yelled
above the rumble of the engine and the
hiss of the air brakes. Jack couldn't hear
what the driver said, but the lorry moved

off faster as the bin man stood out of the way. He came back to talk to Jack.

'There's no room for the driver to pull in here, mate,' he said. 'He's going up to the next turning. You can squeeze past him there.'

'Thank you,' said Jack, with a sigh of relief.

The bin man tapped the side of the van with his hand. He took a step back.

'Good luck, mate. I hope you get there in time.'

The lorry driver waved as Jack squeezed past. Now he found himself in Elm Trees Avenue. It looked exactly the same as Oak Trees Avenue. There were still no trees and

there were still cars parked nose-to-tail
along both sides of the road. But at least he
was moving again.

'This is better,' he thought.

But then ...

Oh, no! A car had stopped in the middle
of the road. Jack jammed on his brakes.
The car was a really old Morris 1000. The

driver's door was wide open and there was no one inside. Where was the driver? Jack looked around in a panic. All he could think about was the poor rabbit.

He beeped his horn.

The net curtains twitched in one of the houses. Someone looked out and then turned away. Jack beeped his horn again. He kept his hand on it. This time the curtains twitched and the window opened.

An old woman stuck her head out.

'Hold on a minute, dear!' she called out. She had a high, thin voice. 'I'll only be a few minutes.'

'I haven't got a few minutes!' yelled Jack. 'It's an emergency!'

The old woman shut the window and came to the front door. She looked at Jack and slowly shook her head.

'You young people,' she tutted. 'Always in such a rush.'

She came down the path towards him like Class 5's tortoise, placing one foot carefully in front of the other, pausing at every step.

'I only popped in to see if my friend Doreen needed anything from the shops. She's got a bad hip, you know ...'

Jack didn't want to be rude but he had to interrupt.

'I'm a plumber,' he said. 'I've got to get to a house that's flooding. There's a pet rabbit trapped inside.'

'Oh, my goodness – I'd better get out of your way!' the old lady said. She sprang into action – ve-ery slo-owly. She opened her handbag and started rummaging through it. Her hands were shaky, like her voice. Her white hair was so thin that the pink skin on the top of her head shone through.

'Now, where did I put my keys?' she mumbled.

She finally found her keys. They were in the car.

'At last!' thought Jack.

The old lady started the engine. The engine stalled. Jack put his forehead on the steering wheel and tried not to say a rude word. Then he got out of the van and moved the car for her.

Jack drove off again. He still couldn't drive very fast between all the parked cars but at least he was moving. He was almost there now.

'This is better,' he thought. He turned into Merrivale Road. But then …

Oh, no! A man in a red running vest and shorts suddenly leapt into the road right

in front of the van. Jack jammed on his brakes.

'What do you think you're doing?' he yelled out of the window. 'Get out of the way! I'm a plumber! This is an emergency!'

'I know,' cried the man. 'I'm the person who rang you!'

· CHAPTER 4 ·

Jack jumped down from the van. He ran round to the back, flung open the doors and grabbed his bag of tools. He splashed up the garden path after the runner. A notice next to the doorbell said:

> # Beware!
> # House rabbit on the loose.
> # Mind your ankles!

'I've been looking through the letterbox,'

the runner said. 'But I still haven't seen the rabbit.'

Jack put down the bag and started searching around for a door key. He looked in all the places people usually hide their spare key. He lifted a plant pot beside the path ... No key. He ran his fingers along the gutter on the porch ... No key. He felt around inside the letterbox. Sometimes people tied their key to a piece of string so that you could pull it through the letterbox. But there was no string and no key.

'What are we going to do?' said the runner
They could hear the water sloshing against
the inside of the door.

'There's only one thing we can do,' said
Jack.

He opened his tool bag and took out a
heavy lever. He stuck the lever between the
edge of the door and the frame. He pushed.
Nothing happened. He pushed harder. There
was a cracking sound.

All of a sudden, the door flew open. It
crashed against the wall of the house and a
great wave of water came rushing out. The
runner jumped out of the way. Jack grabbed
his tool bag. He waded into the house, with
the water swirling around his legs.

The kitchen was at the end of the hall.
Jack headed straight towards it – but then he

stopped in the doorway. Water was gushing out of a broken pipe next to the washing machine. It was like the super-jet at the swimming pool. It might be strong enough to knock him off his feet.

But he couldn't turn back now. He battled through the gushing water towards the broken pipe. He had to half close his eyes against the spray. Could he fix it?

Yes! He did it! The water stopped gushing. There was just a little trickle. He would have to mend that later but first he had something much more important to do.

The rabbit hutch was floating upside down. Bags of crisps bobbed around it like bright jellyfish. The water level was dropping now. Jack searched the cupboards and high surfaces.

When he turned round again the hutch was lying on the wet kitchen floor. It looked like an old box washed up on the beach by the sea. Full of dread, he opened the hutch

door. The rabbit was not there.

The runner picked his way into the kitchen, trying not to get his expensive running shoes wet. He was carrying an old soggy blanket. Jack looked again and saw it wasn't a blanket. It was a half-drowned rabbit.

He was very big for a rabbit. He was nearly as big as Porridge. His chocolate-brown fur was soaking wet. His eyes were closed and big drips were falling from the ends of his long drooping ears.

'He needs a vet,' the runner said. 'You'll have to take him in your van.'

They found some towels in the bathroom and wrapped the rabbit up in them. Then the runner carried him out to the van. Jack opened the passenger door.

The runner shook his head and walked round to the back of the van.

'We should put him in the back,' he said. 'He might perk up when he's dried out a bit. He might start hopping around.'

'You're right,' said Jack. That could happen. He remembered the time Nico fell off the trampoline. He went so droopy they rushed him off to hospital. But half-way there, he suddenly perked up and started jumping on the seat, yelling 'Dampoline, dampoline!'

So Jack dashed back inside and fetched some cushions. He made a cosy bed in the bath that was still in the back of the van, and the runner put the rabbit in it.

The runner waved goodbye and ran off up the road. Jack drove as fast as he could to the vet's surgery. He couldn't hear any noise from the back of the van. Maybe the rabbit was better. Maybe he was worse. It was horrible not knowing.

Jack pulled in at the vet's. He jumped out. As he opened the back door, the rabbit sat up. His wet fur was fluffy in patches where it was starting to dry off. Jack picked him up and carried him inside.

'I've just rescued this rabbit from a flood,' he explained to the girl at the desk.

'You'd better go straight through,' she said. 'He mustn't catch a chill.'

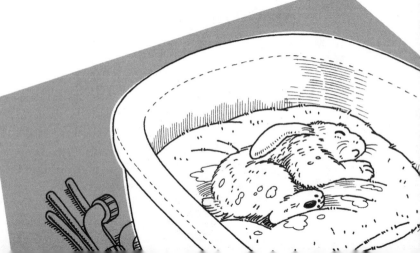

The vet was cleaning her examination table with a special wipe. When she saw the rabbit, she smiled.

'I know this little fellow!' she said. 'He comes to me for all his check-ups.'
She patted the examination table with her hand, and Jack carefully put the rabbit down.

The vet got out her stethoscope.

'OK, Harry,' she said to the rabbit. 'I'm

just going to listen to your heart.'

Harry sniffed at the stethoscope as the vet put it against his side. She listened. She nodded to herself.

'I think he's going to be all right,' she told Jack. 'Rabbits don't like water. He's very lucky that you got to him in time.'

The vet said she wanted to keep an eye on Harry for a few hours.

'Leave him with me,' she said. 'I'll phone his family and ask them to come in and pick him up later.'

Jack went back out to his van. He felt good. He felt great! This time, he stuck to the High Street, stop, start, stop, start. He wasn't in a hurry any more. He had finished his adventure. In no time at all, he found himself back at the car supermarket.

· CHAPTER 5 ·

Jack drew the shape of the big white van and went over it in black felt-tip pen. He was using light blue paper so that his white colouring pencil would show up on it. He opened his new car-shaped pencil case and took out the white.

Dad was sitting at his desk filling in some forms.

'So you liked that van, then?' he said.

Jack only made posters of the cars he liked. Dad said they were trying to sell cars, not put people off. It wouldn't do to pin up a poster that said, 'This car is very dull and boring!'

Jack said, 'Yes. It really is very versatile. You could carry a new bath in it. You could put your heavy tool-bag in the back. You could even take a half-drowned rabbit to the vet's.'

'A half-drowned rabbit?' said Dad, in surprise.

Jack went on colouring. *Shika-shika* went

the pencil on the pale blue paper.

'Well, if a pipe burst then a house could get flooded, couldn't it? And if there was a rabbit inside, someone would have to rescue it.'

'Ah,' said Dad.

Shika-shika went the pencil on the pale blue paper. The colouring-in was going really well. You could hardly see the pencil marks at all.

'Actually, Jack,' Dad said, 'if a pipe burst in a house there wouldn't really be that kind of flood. Not deep water sloshing about.'

Jack frowned.

Shika-shika.

He thought that Dad was wrong.

Shika-shika.

He put his pencil down and sat back on his heels.

'But I've seen flooded houses on the news,' he said.

Dad told him floods like that only happened when there was lots of rain and rivers overflowed. A burst pipe wasn't like a river. The water wouldn't gush out fast enough to make a full-on flood.

Jack thought about this for a minute.

'Then why have we got 'emergency plumber' on that list of numbers beside the phone?' he said. 'If your house wouldn't flood, what's the emergency?'

'I didn't say it wouldn't flood,' Dad pointed out. 'I said it wouldn't be so deep you could drown. If you had a leaky pipe you'd need a plumber straight away before all your carpets got ruined.'

'Oh,' said Jack.

Rescuing carpets wasn't exactly as exciting as rescuing a drowning person or pet.

'And not just your carpets,' said Dad. 'All your special things. For you, it might be your road maps and pictures and cars. Imagine.'

Jack thought of his bedroom and the

birthday presents lined up on the floor beside his bed. He hadn't even had a chance to play with them yet. He imagined them all soggy and spoiled by water from a leaky pipe in the bathroom.

Pets and people mattered most, but special things mattered too. 'When I've finished this poster,' thought Jack, 'I'll go back and have another plumber adventure, only this time I'll rescue someone's special things.'

Jack went happily back to his colouring. He thought about all the special things he could rescue. An old person's photo album. A pop star's piano. A baby's favourite cuddly toy. He finished the picture and then wrote underneath it:

Ford Transit. This is a very versatile van.

You can carry all sorts of things in it, for eksample heavy tools and baths.

'Can I go and play in the van again now?' Jack asked his dad.

But before his dad could answer, they heard a shriek outside. They looked round and saw Nico. He was smacking his hands on the glass door, yelling, 'Dada! Dada! Dack!' Amber appeared behind him. She took his hand and pushed the door open. It didn't look as if ballet had cheered her up much. Mum came in after them.

'Miss Marietta said my plie was wonky,' Amber grumbled.

'What's a plie?' asked Dad.

'Phh!' Amber said. She threw herself down on one of the sofas.

'AND she told me off for having a hole in my tights,' Amber grumbled.

Nico tried to climb up beside her. She pushed him away.

'AND there's no class next week. I'm going to be stuck at home! It's going to be *so* boring!'

Mum tried to ignore her.

'Ready for lunch?' she asked Jack.

'Nearly,' he said. 'Can I just have a minute to finish my poster?'

'Phh!' went Amber.

Jack wrote something else on his poster. He showed it to Dad. Dad smiled. He showed it to Mum. Mum smiled. He showed it to Amber. He got ready to run!

Ford Transit.

Ford Transit. This is a very versatile van. You can carry all sorts of things in it, for eksample heavy tools and baths.

You could even put your grumpy sister in the back. Then you wouldn't have to hear her grumbling all the way home!

Jack.

Amber glared at the poster. She made a grab for it to tear it up, but Jack whisked it away. He ran over to his 'wall of cars' and held it up in the gap where the Rugged Range-Rover had been.

'Can I have some drawing pins, Dad?' asked Jack.

The Alien looked as if she might explode.

'You're not going to let him pin that up!' she cried.

'Why not?' said Dad, handing Jack some pins. 'It's only a bit of fun.'

Amber made a noise like a strangled hippo and stormed out of the showroom.

Mum sighed.

'What a morning!' she said.

She looked back at Jack's poster, in the middle of his 'wall of cars'.

'You know what?' she said. 'I think I'd like to buy that versatile van!'

Dad grinned at Jack.

'Another cracking poster!' he said. 'I always say your posters sell more cars than I do!'

Look out for more of Car-mad Jack's adventures in the following books:

The Speedy Sports Car
The Motorbike in the Mountains
The Marvellous Minibus
The Taxi About Town
The Rugged Off-roader